The Damned

The Damned

Iridescent Toad Publishing

Iridescent Toad Publishing.

Cover by M.Y. Cover Design.

First edition. ISBN 978-1-8380186-6-5

*Extra special thanks to Tanya Lee Clark
for helping me bring this book to life.*

Chapter One

The crisp cold air snapped at my wings. I extended each slick black feather into place, letting the wind glide over me as I sliced through the sky. I loved the winter and the peaceful stillness that came with it.

Traversing the thin layer between the afterlife and the land of the living wasn't something that I did often. It wasn't a difficult journey, at least not for me, it just wasn't one that I enjoyed taking. I preferred to keep my distance from the living, breathing humans that seemed to cause increasingly more annoyance with each passing moment. But on this night I had something to take care of; something that wouldn't be resolved without my help.

My black eyes gleaned beneath the moonlight as I plunged below the lingering clouds and made my way towards the house. It was once *her* house, but now it belonged only to the man I had planned to see. The smells of the town drifted upon the air and tempted me with the delights of the living; warm bread, pungent alcohol, and even the wafting scent of spicy sausages that had crackled to a crispy skin on an open flame. As tempting as they all were, no earthly pleasures appealed to me enough. There was only one thing that drove me forward and I knew that the sooner I completed my task, the sooner I would be able to leave.

The house was small; tattered on the outside but cosy on the inside – at least from what I could tell from outside the window. When my talons touched down on the wooden window ledge, I could already feel the heat from inside the humble dwelling permeating through the glass panes as I peered into the house.

A robin, or a sparrow perhaps, might have pressed their belly against the glass to warm up. I wasn't interested in being warm though. The snowflakes falling around me dusted everything in a white veil. It emphasised my ebony appearance. Fortunately for me, the curious little town was comfortable with its dreary and almost macabre appearance; a perched raven would draw no attention at all.

Through the window I could see a man inside the house. He was making tea with a tarnished silver kettle. I watched him put it under the running water of the sink. He gazed vacantly at the wall in front of him as the water overflowed from the small vessel. This man and his misery was my reason for visiting the house.

When the man realised that the kettle was over-filled, he turned the tap off. He set the kettle on the stove burner without thinking to turn it on, and walked back over to the living room to sit down on a hard, wooden chair in the corner of the room.

He sat in bewildered anticipation, opening his mouth to talk as if there was someone else there with him. But then he thought better of it and closed his lips together as he shook his head. It was a sad sight to see, this lonely soul devoid of companionship and longing for a lost love. I knew that there had once been a woman here with him, and that upon her death, he had been heartbroken. There were many questions surrounding the woman's death, none of which I knew the answers to, even though I had speculated from time to time.

The man got up from the chair and disappeared into another room for a few moments before arriving back with an armful of books. He dropped all but one of them onto the floor as he slumped back down into the chair. He cracked open the binding of the book in his hands and began reading the pages.

I called upon my keen vision to make out the titles on the book covers. The compendiums were all tales of lost lore and stories of forgotten love. It was the reading material of a lonely heart. I watched the man's chest heave as he cried upon the turning of an occasional page. The books failed to distract him from his heartache. I endeavoured to remind myself that words held power, whether written or spoken. Even great masterpieces of romance though, could not sway the heart of a grieving man whose loss felt unbearable and desperate.

Letting him sit there and sink into his sorrows would surely not solve anything. I had to intervene. The moon was now behind the clouds. It made the night pitch black even with the tiny glow of streetlamps off in the distance. It was the perfect darkness to match my feathers. I flew swiftly and silently to the door of the house and tapped my beak against the wood seven times. For a moment, I heard nothing stir. But then the door creaked open and the man stood before me, staring out into the night.

With two hops to the side of the door, I was hidden from sight. I watched the man and heard him call out into the cold air.

"Lenore?" he asked. "Lenore? Is that you?"

It sounded more like a quiet plea than a question.

The man tried to scan the darkness with his weary

eyes, but there was nothing there for him to see. I could see the tears in them and for a moment, I felt guilty about having disturbed him with false hope.

When the door closed, I flew back to the windowsill. Perhaps, in time, I could just let the man be and the situation would resolve itself.

I watched as he walked to the stove. He remembered to turn the burner on for his kettle and then sat down in the wooden chair. This time, he didn't bother to pick up one of the books from the floor. Instead, he stared out into the room, looking at a portrait on the far wall. Lenore. She was beautiful; dark hair cascading down against her shoulders and equally dark eyes that seemed to look back at him – almost hauntingly. Her plump breasts were alluring.

The man softly rubbed his hand over his crotch in remembrance of the intimate moments they'd shared. It was uncomfortable for me to observe.

The longer the man stared at the portrait, the more his longing for Lenore grew, until at last, he loosened his trousers and thrust his hand inside to pull out his fully hardened cock. My black marble eyes grew wide as he began to push and pull his hand against himself in guttural pleasure. His mouth hung open and his eyes remained fixed on the image of Lenore as he stroked himself. He was oblivious to the fact that there was an onlooker peering through his window. Even if he had known, it possibly wouldn't have made him stop anyway. After all, what would the opinion of a bird matter to him?

Feeling restless from the man's act, I shifted anxiously on the ledge, my talons digging into the wood. I wanted to bash my tiny head against the window to discourage him from his lustful indulgence. I knew it wouldn't break the sexual connection that he still felt towards Lenore though. I would need to be smarter about it, even if it would pain me to the point of wanting to peck the man's eyes from his skull.

As the kettle began to whistle, the man too, began to peak. His body convulsed into a fit of gratification. He wiped the tip of his wet cock with his sleeve, pulled his trousers back up, and went to remove the screaming kettle from the stove.

I had never understood why humans considered themselves to be a superior species; I found them, in every way, to be wholly desperate and disgusting. The man poured his tea and placed it on a small table next to his chair. He then reached down to pick up the next book he would read. It would be a cycle; reading, staring forlornly at the portrait of his lost love, and appeasing his physical desires.

It had become clear to me that the man would not be capable of ending it on his own; I would have to help him. But in such a way that he would not get wise to what I was capable of.

I shook my head, clearing the snow from my feathers, but really it was my thoughts that I needed to shake off. I tapped my beak against the window, sharply enough that the sound echoed throughout the small home.

The man immediately looked up towards the window. He saw nothing but the blackness outside. My dark silhouette must have camouflaged against the backdrop of the night. With less hope than before, the man went to the window and pressed his face against it to see what had made the noise. Still he saw nothing. He opened the window in swift preparation to scream out into the emptiness – all in the feeble hope of being able to hear his pain echoed back to him. Before any sound could come from his throat though, I lifted my feet from the wood and took to my wings.

I flew into the room with such force that it startled the man and knocked him backwards to the ground. As I looked for a place to land, he watched me circle just below the ceiling.

"What is this?!" he shouted. "What manner of night visitor are you?"

I chose to perch on a bust that was resting on the fireplace mantle. My talons scraped against the stone as I gripped it and spread my wings wide to make myself seem powerful and haunting. I looked down at the man with foreboding eyes. I wanted to swallow his attention and command the room.

As the man rose to his feet, he quickly went to shut the window. Perhaps he didn't want me to leave. I may have been merely a bird to him, and it may have been an unusual and unnerving occurrence but the man had received no visitors since Lenore's passing and he was lonely beyond measure. Even a raven would be a welcome companion for him at this point. I wasn't pleased with my incarceration, but I wasn't intimidated by it either. I had a job to do. I would get it done and I would find a way to leave this place.

The man approached me slowly.

"What is your name?" he asked.

My name? I thought to myself. With the exception of the one soul that I was anxious to return to, no one knew my name. This was my chance to begin my game with the man. I needed to choose my word carefully, for it would be the word to send hope spiralling from the man's mind – all to cut the ties with his lost love. It would be the word to drive him mad.

"I ask you again," the man said with increasing desperation. "What is your name, creature?"

At that moment, I wished I was in my other form; I would have liked to have coupled my word with a devilish grin.

"Nevermore," I called in response.

As I repeated the word and tried out the feeling of it on my tongue, all he could do was watch.

"*Nevermore?*" he said as he pondered its meaning. "How is it that a bird can know such a word?"

"Nevermore," I said again.

"Are you a messenger from my love, sent from beyond the grave to reach me? What could she mean by sending me such a word?"

"Nevermore."

"Or are you just a bird that has escaped a cruel master, here to join another broken soul in dire sorrow?"

"Nevermore."

I remained steadily affixed to the top of the bust as he repeated the word without pause.

He tried to move closer to me, reaching out a hand

to stroke my wing. I shouted the word at him in a way that sounded more like a human than a bird. The man quickly drew his hand back and stepped away. I flapped my wings and looked at him menacingly. He proceeded to pace the floor, rubbing his jaw and unsure of how to interpret my presence.

"Surely if Lenore had sent you, she would have sent you with a message," he said. "A sign perhaps – something that would bring me peace and comfort and would let me know that she is waiting for me, until we can be reunited in the afterlife and be together again."

I looked at him with both pity and impatience.

"Tell me raven, what message do you bring for me?"

"Nevermore."

A slight annoyance began to grow within his voice.

"Do you know only one word? How am I to decipher a message from my love if you can utter only a single word? Or perhaps you are just a stupid bird who has only one word in its head to repeat. Is this the case: are you mimicking the word of someone you've fled? Does this word mean more to you than it does to me?"

I sat in silence as I watched the man's pace quicken and draw a tighter circle across the floor. I wondered how long this would take.

The man approached me again and raised a hand as if about to strike me. I simply continued to stare at him with frozen eyes. I opened my beak to speak the word again.

"Nevermore."

The man's hand froze in the air and the colour drained from his face.

"Forgive me," he whispered sweetly. "You are not a simple bird. I can see that. You are a messenger and I must throw light on your message instead of trying to silence you. Forgive me spirit."

Oh this is fun, I thought. *Now he thinks I'm a spirit!*

18

Chapter Two

There was a chair in the room, one that used to belong to Lenore. It was her favourite chair and she would always sit on its plush cushion to read by the fireplace. The man would bring her cups of tea as she read. She would rest her head against the soft back, sometimes falling asleep mid-page and letting the book drop to her lap. The man would sit and watch her as she slept and would think of how lucky he was to have found her in this world.

The chair had remained in the corner of the room. The man went to reach for it. He pulled it in front of the hearth to face me on the mantle.

"Let's have a conversation," he said to me. "You and I."

The heat from the fire warmed the chair and made the scent of Lenore's perfume – which still resided in its fabric – rise in the room. I knew that scent. The man and I each had our own different memories of Lenore – some more startling than others.

"Where are you from?" he asked me, speaking as if we were colleagues.

"Nevermore."

"Since that is not a place, I will take your answer as literally as I can think it to be. You must be from a place that no longer exists. Perhaps you have already died and have been reincarnated as a bird? By chance, are you my dearest Lenore?"

"Nevermore."

"My Lenore would not leave me with so many questions. She would answer me to satisfaction. I think you are not her at all," he said, disheartened again.

I stared back at the pitifully disillusioned man before me. I made a sound that resembled a small laugh. *You do not know her at all*, I thought.

"You are a messenger, that much I know. What does your message mean? Does it mean that I will be lonely no more? Or that you will be the last soul that I speak with before I am nevermore to be heard from again? Are you a harbinger of death so that I may join my lost love once and for all?"

"Nevermore."

My word bounced off the walls of the small house,

sounding as though it had been said four times more.

"If you are not death, and you are not my Lenore, then what are you? Just a stupid bird that knows one word. One cryptic and taunting word that eats at my brain."

The man stood up from the chair and went to fetch something from the bedroom. He returned with an armful of trinkets and artefacts that had once belonged to Lenore.

He held up a locket for me to see.

"See this one?" he said feverishly. "I gave this to her on our first anniversary. It opens to hold a picture inside, but it is empty now. It was supposed to hold a picture of our first child, but that was not meant to be."

I watched carefully as he spilled the contents in his arms onto the chair in front of us.

"Yes, you like shiny things, don't you?" he teased. "I've heard that about ravens, that they are attracted to pretty things."

Well, that part he has right, I thought.

"And that they will bring you gifts if you make friends with them. Perhaps you'll start bringing me gifts soon too."

The man had a twisted smile on his face that indicated he was losing his grip on reality.

We aren't friends.

The man waved a glass bottle over his head. The light pink liquid inside sloshed around and the same scent that was imbued into the chair filled the room. It made the bristles at the opening of my nostrils flare.

"And this," he continued. "Lenore loved this perfume. I can still smell her scent in this house."

So can I.

"She was a beautiful woman. Pretty, and kind, and even though she would get lost in her books for hours at a time, I was never lonely when she was here. I am lonely now though. So very, very lonely."

I adjusted my talons on the stone bust, a spot I had chosen purposefully. The bust was of Athena, the Greek goddess of wisdom – an ironic ornament in the man's home considering his state of mind.

"Why do you sit there looking down at me from that bust? Do you think yourself to be superior and more knowledgeable than I? Tell me raven, what thoughts rest in that tiny head of yours that deem you worthy to sit upon my mantle in judgement?"

"Nevermore."

A fire of rage burned in the man's eyes as he hurled Lenore's locket towards me. Perhaps he did it in the hope of being able to knock me from my place. It was easy to spread my wings wide to keep my balance. The locket hit against my breast.

The wider I spread my wings, the larger I looked. The man was already in such decline that it wasn't difficult to intimidate him.

He lowered his eyes and raised his palms up as if to apologise. He then brushed the items from the chair and sat back down. I watched as he leaned his head back and closed his eyes. A flood of memories rushed to him as he allowed himself to sink into the soft chair. He was clearly overwhelmed by his sorrow.

When he opened his eyes again, he was met with none other than my unchanging stare. He sighed.

"Are you going to leave me too?" he asked.

"Nevermore."

"I suppose you will. I doubt that you would want to stay."

The man's demeanour seemed to change abruptly from anger to meekness.

"Tell me raven, have you ever loved anyone?"

"Nevermore," I answered.

"I thought not. Birds cannot feel passion and companionship in the way that people can. You would have no idea what I am talking about."

How wrong you are.

"I try to think of what death will be like and what will come after it. Do you think I will see my dearest Lenore in the afterlife?"

"Nevermore."

The pitch in the man's voice became higher in a state of desperation.

"What does that mean?" he begged. "Do you mean that I'll never see her again? Just answer me damned bird! I cannot go without knowing. You will tire of keeping to your one word before I tire of my questions – that much I can promise you!"

I sighed, my bony rib cage moving beneath my feathery breast. I didn't have time for this, nor did I want to delay my return.

"I have read that ravens have one eye in the land

of the living and one in the land of the dead. Is this true?"

"Nevermore."

"If I plucked out your eyes, would I be able to see my precious Lenore beyond the veil of death?"

"Nevermore."

"Why are you here?!"

The man's face flushed beet red as his temper enraged him again.

"Nevermore."

This time, I took flight as I called the tormenting word out into the air. I circled around the room, dropping low to the man's head as I called.

"Nevermore. Nevermore."

The word seemed to surround the man from every available space inside the house. He reached up to try and grab hold of me, unsure of what he would actually do thereafter anyway. I was much too swift for him, evading his grasp each time I circled near.

On my last turn around the man's head, I reached a talon down towards him. It swiped a gash alongside his cheek. He winced and shouted a profanity at me as he slapped his hand against the open cut.

He ran into the bathroom to see the wound and dressed it with antiseptic and a bandage.

When he returned to the room, it may have been in the hope that I had gone (even though it was he who had closed the window). I was still there though, sitting on the bust just like before.

The candles in the room were dying down, as was the fire in the hearth. The dim glow of light cast oversized shadows onto the walls. With my glinting eyes and spread wings, I cast the biggest shadow of all. It encased the room in my presence. I must have looked demonic and monstrous to the man as he looked up at me.

"You have come to serve me with judgement," he wept as he knelt before me.

I had pitied him slightly at first, but the lingering voice in my head was calling to me to return. It was a waste of time – and wearing – to stay here in this hovel with a madman.

"Stay with me," the man called to me. "If you cannot be my Lenore, perhaps you could at least be my companion."

"Nevermore."

"Then, demon spirit, if you are neither, do what you have to do; carry me to the great death beyond this life so that I may be with my love once more."

"Nevermore."

The man's pupils shook as he stared up, infuriated at my insistence. He stood and flapped his arms as if they were wings. He started to run around the edge of the room in circles as he feigned being a bird himself.

"Nevermore, nevermore, nevermore," he shrieked and laughed, trying to mock me.

He has truly lost his mind, I thought as I followed his movements. *At least it has worked, and he is near the edge of madness. Perhaps now he will forget about Lenore and I can be on my way.*

The man started to pull all of his clothes off as he continued to caw and squawk, until he stood before me completely naked. For a moment, it looked as though he was going to gratify himself again. I felt my patience wane. He did something entirely unexpected though. He threw open the front door and ran outside – barefoot and naked – into the cold air.

He ran only a few steps before his feet became numb. He then toppled over, letting his body sink into the snow as more of it drifted onto him. I flew out to look at him and saw within moments that his lips were turning blue. The tips of his fingers and toes were turning a blistering red from the freezing cold.

"Nevermore," I screeched loudly.

It proved to be a futile attempt to rouse the man. Completely ignoring me, he stared blankly up into the night sky. I had hoped that in a swift action, he would have darted back inside the house. I didn't want him to die.

"Nevermore!" I called again.

I even went so far as to land on the man's bare chest to screech into his face. He had lost consciousness though. He was motionless in the heap of snow. Even then though, a small and perverse-looking grin edged on the corners of his lips.

I'd had enough. I began to peck at the man's chest until it was impossible for him to ignore me. As much as he tried to swat me away, I stayed and continued pecking as I called the fateful word.

"Nevermore!"

Eventually, between the cold and the pain of my pecking – and the even more painful sound of the word being called – the man stood up and ran back inside his house. Almost slamming the door, he wasn't quite fast enough to prevent me from following him back inside.

He shook with cold and with fear. He looked up at Lenore's portrait on the wall.

"She would be quite disappointed in me now, wouldn't she?" he asked.

"Nevermore," I replied.

I didn't understand how any woman could have ever been in love with such a pathetic creature as this man.

He slowly put his clothes back on and went to the kitchen to heat up some soup. Try as he might, he could not let go of her. Even though it caused him pain and madness, he held on to his remembrance of Lenore in a desperately masochistic attempt to keep her with him – if only in memory.

When he returned to the living room, the man was carrying two bowls of soup. He set one down on the floor several paces away from the chair. He then took the other one in his hands as he sat back down against the soft cushion.

"It's for you," he said to me. "I suppose you might have just saved my life out there."

I couldn't deny that I was hungry. And even though I enjoyed the cold weather, there was a different kind of cold – possibly one caused by the dreariness of the situation – that made me think about how great the hot soup would feel sliding down my gullet. I swooped down gracefully from the mantle and stood beside the bowl, eyeing the man in the chair suspiciously.

He laughed, but kindly so. He bent down and swapped the bowl on the floor with the one in his hands.

"Here," he said. "You do not trust me, and I can see why. But if I had poisoned the soup, I wouldn't be eating it myself, would I?"

I looked down at the soup in the bowl in front of me. I dipped my beak in and had a little taste. It was good.

For a few quiet moments, the two of us enjoyed the soup in silence as we kept our thoughts to ourselves. The man had swung his mood so many times already that I didn't trust who he would become once he'd finished with his soup. As soon as I had finished mine, I flew back up to sit on top of the bust again. The man collected both of the bowls to take to the sink. As he was washing them clean, I could hear him crying.

Chapter Three

There were a few things about Lenore's death that troubled me. The cause had been declared as tuberculosis, but there had been no autopsy. Everyone in the drab little town went along with the coroner's claim without question. Nobody seemed willing to talk about it further.

The town was small and bleak. I was very familiar with each nook and cranny of its architecture – both humble and grand – that lined the streets. I had kept an eye on this town even before I had known Lenore. Once I had seen her though, everything had changed.

All of the townsfolk regarded the man as some sort of recluse; a writer who rarely left his home, and when he did it was always with Lenore on his arm. She was much friendlier than he was, always saying hello to people on the street and smiling warmly with the radiant smile that had first attracted my attention.

I felt as though I was the only one who found the town's indifference towards Lenore's death unsettling. I tried not to think about it, for I was here with the man for a very different reason; to help him let go of Lenore. It made no difference whether his tears were from guilt, sorrow, or a combination of the two. All that mattered was for him to not hold onto her in his heart forever.

My perception of time was very different to the man's. Time passed differently for him – so much so that it was less on his thoughts than mine. Each moment that I spent with him seemed like it was a moment too much.

Once he had finished washing the bowls and had dried his eyes with a towel, he came back to sit in his wooden chair in the corner of the room. He picked up another book and buried his nose in it, seeming to ignore my presence entirely.

What is this? I thought. I didn't allow myself to hope that the man had simply pushed aside his grief. The ordeal wasn't over.

He continued to read as I sat patiently and waited. I could only look at my surroundings at length and preen my feathers to a glossy shine so much before growing unbearably restless. Just as I was about to pluck a feather to drop on the ground to get the man's attention, he spoke.

"Perhaps the best cure for a poisoned and broken heart would be to find another woman to bandage the wound," he said forlornly.

Now we are getting somewhere.

He looked up at me from his book.

"If you were me, would you do such a thing?" he asked. "Would you find another woman to heal your broken heart? Or would it pain my dear Lenore to watch over me and see that I had moved on? Love is supposed to be eternal – but I am not sure if it should exceed death and carry on through it."

"Nevermore," I called.

"Perhaps I should sleep on it."

The man set his book down and made his way towards the bedroom.

"Nevermore," I called after him.

I looked between his disappearing presence and the closed window. There was no time for sleep, only time to reconcile his past in order that I could leave and fly back to where I had come from.

The man waved his hand in the air behind him as if to disregard my cawing. He closed his bedroom door tightly, leaving me alone in the greater part of the house with a dwindling fire which was nearly out.

There is nothing for me to do but wait, I thought as I hopped down from the bust and walked across the floor of the house to the strewn pile of books by the man's chair. I flipped some of the covers open with my beak and looked inside at the words. They looked as if they had been scrawled by talons dipped in ink. The stories inside were dark and heartbreaking, a perfect mirror of the man's mood.

I flapped my wings up to hover in front of Lenore's portrait. I gazed into her deeply painted eyes. They resembled caverns. I then flew to the windowsill and stared outside. The snow was still falling but it was now a mixture of rain and slush in place of the fluffy snowflakes that had been there earlier. The drops were heavy and made a small pattering sound against the window as the wind blew.

How I longed to be free of this house and to be flying through the wet cool air back to where I belonged. How I wished the man wasn't so stubborn and disillusioned. I knew that I could always fly up and out through the chimney once the fire had died completely and the smoke had cooled. But I also knew that if I didn't finish my task, there would never be peace for the man. That would mean that there would never be peace for me. I too, was weary. It had been a difficult evening. I had low expectations for what the morning would have in store.

I flew from the windowsill and onto the cushion of Lenore's chair. I walked a few small circles around the fabric, my talons catching on it as I moved. I then sat and buried my head in my feathers. As I slept, Lenore's scent wafted up through the cushions around me.

Dreams were a frequent occurrence for me, so much so that it often felt as though my dream state and waking state were an interwoven mix of realities. On this occasion, I dreamt of Lenore and the man inside the house. In my dream, the man seemed infatuated. He followed Lenore around the house like a lost puppy, waiting expectantly for her return each time she ventured out into the town alone.

I knew of Lenore's day trips into the town, her visits to the market and how she would stop to listen to the street performers and leave coins for them in their collection buckets. I knew of those things because I would see her as I soared through the sky above, sometimes landing nearby to watch her more closely. I had never known why the man didn't attend the outings with her, or what he got up to while he was alone by himself.

The man dreamt that night too. He dreamt of a

black shadow that followed him everywhere; a shadow that looked like the shape of his lost love. He chased the dark shadow from room to room, calling Lenore's name and trying to grab onto her form each time he got close enough to do so. The shadow simply dissipated into the air though, leaving his fingers to grab onto themselves instead. The faster the man chased the shadow, the smaller and more elusive it became, until finally it was nothing more than a dark wisp hovering in the corner by the hearth. As the man walked slowly towards it, the wisp vanished, leaving only one long black feather on the floor in its place.

The man woke in a sweat and sat straight up in his bed. He flung the sheets off his legs and raced to the bedroom door. When he opened it and saw me on the chair of his deceased love, he shouted at me in a delusional episode. I jumped with a start. I got straight to my feet and spread my wings.

"Lenore!" he called out. "Lenore it is you, isn't it?"

"Nevermore!" I called in return.

As my eyes fixed onto the man, I could see that he was most definitely not in his right mind.

"It *is* you! Why do you deny me, my love?"

The man lunged forwards as if to grab me, but he wasn't fast enough. I was already in flight.

"Come back, come back to me!" he screamed.

I flew furiously around the room, trying to avoid capture. I knew he was unhinged. I didn't want to end up with a snapped neck and made into a stew.

"I am sorry, my love," the man cried out. "I blame myself for your death and it should not have happened."

I froze mid-air before landing on the bust, boring a menacing glare into the man.

"What is it that you want me to do in order to make it up to you? I will do anything, anything you ask. Just show me a sign and soothe my troubled soul with your presence. I will love you forever and always and I will never let you go again. Just give me a sign and I will do whatever you ask of me. *Please* Lenore, I'm begging you!"

It is me that you should be begging now, I thought. I felt my anger swell within me as I raised my neck high and bellowed the word at the man.

"NEVERMORE!"

He covered his ears at the sound and must have sensed the violent rage stirring within my soul. He backed away in fear.

"If you are Lenore, then I no longer recognise you.

Death has turned your spirit evil and vile. And if it is not you, then you have sent a demon in your place to torment me further instead of leaving me to my own quiet suffering. I will have no more of you."

The man went to the window and opened it wide. I was free to leave. He then walked back into his bedroom and closed the door behind him.

Although the temptation to take flight and leave this world was intoxicating, I stayed. The man's erratic behaviour had given me enough insight to know that he could easily change his mind and mood again and emerge from his bedroom, pining once more for his lost love. I could not leave until certain that the man would sever his mournful, never-ending remembrance. I sat on the bust of the Greek goddess and watched the sleet fall outside of the open window.

When morning came, the light was barely brighter than the night had been, all thanks to the thick clouds and cold rain. The house was cold from the outside breeze blowing in and the lack of fire in the hearth. The man had not yet emerged from his room.

If only Lenore could see this place now, I thought to myself. *She would be easily rid of this house and this man if she knew how demented he had become without her.*

"Good morning, bird," the man said casually as he opened his bedroom door and stepped out. "I must say that I am surprised to see you are still here. Perhaps you have been sent to spy on me. Are you karma's form, here to serve me my equal share of punishment?"

"Nevermore," I replied.

"Whatever," he said. "The punishment I give myself does more damage than anything that you could ever dish out."

He set the kettle on the stove and turned on the burner to make his morning tea. Then he walked to stand in front of me, apparently not feeling the cold chill in the house as he stood before the empty fireplace.

"I have decided that I will kill myself," he announced. "Then I'll be able to join my love in the afterlife."

No you fool, I thought. *That's not how it works.*

"I have no one left here to bury me. I will burn instead of being placed in the earth. You will carry my ashes in your beak to my Lenore. There, in the afterlife, we shall be reunited and happy once more. Will you do this for me, my feathered friend?"

"Nevermore!" I shouted in warning.

"We are obviously at a standstill for words, you and I. So I will just have to take you on your honour that you will carry out my wishes."

The man went to retrieve his tea before coming back to start a new fire in the hearth. With the window still open, once the fire started to blaze there was a delightful mix of cold and warm air swirling around the room. The rain had stopped, leaving behind only an overcast day.

He sipped his tea as he stood in his robe looking at Lenore's portrait, mumbling under his breath about tragic love stories and how death met the end of every single classic work of literature in which love was a key theme. He compared himself and Lenore to the works of Shakespeare and laughed to himself about how much darker and more deserving his death would be than Romeo's. I was convinced at this point that it wouldn't be possible to bring the man back from the lunacy that his grief had plunged him into.

Once he'd finished his tea, he set the cup down and went to pick up his books from the floor. He walked over to the crackling fire in the hearth with several volumes gathered in his arms. Sitting down in front of it, he dipped the first book into the flame. I watched and cawed with wide-eyed fear.

As soon as the pages were abundantly ignited, the man withdrew the book and set it beside him. He did the same with all of the books until he was surrounded by a burning ring of them. The flames eased nearer and nearer to his robe.

I cawed and screeched furiously as I flew overhead and slammed my wings against the air with each powerful beat.

"Nevermore! Nevermore!" I screamed as I watched the fire grow taller.

This is madness. He intends to burn his house down with himself inside.

Although I hated a great many things about the man, I pitied him and his heartbreak. I would have stopped the flames if I could have done. I didn't want him to meet his end in this way.

As soon as several flames were on the man's robe, it took only a matter of seconds for the fire to consume everything around it. I flew quickly out of the window and perched far enough away from the house that I could watch it burn from a safe distance. The reaching crimson flames reflected in my eyes.

The town had only a small fire truck. It arrived much too late to do anything other than wet down the already smouldering ashes – they were all that was left of the house by then. I watched throughout the day as various town officials came to document what had happened. Various scavengers and street urchins came to pick through the cooling ash for anything left that was of value.

When night fell and the people had all gone back to their own homes, I flew to the rubble to take a look around. There was nothing left of the man apart from a few scattered and blackened teeth. There was nothing left of the house – or its contents – except for a cracked and brittle section of the stone bust that had rested on the fireplace mantle. Everything else was no more, including the lingering plight of the man.

I knew that the man's delusional hopes of being reunited with his love would not happen, but at least he would find the silent peace of nothingness in his death. No more pining after lost love, no more anything. It was all over now and I could finally return home.

I sighed and shook the ash from my wings as I prepared to take flight. I was both relieved and saddened by the man's fate. I certainly owed him no kindness, and an end was exactly what I had come here seeking. But still, Lenore had loved the man once, so there must have been a part of him that had been worth something.

"Shoo!"

It was a street urchin shouting at me. He waved his hands around to get me to leave so that he could rummage through the wreckage once more under the cover of darkness.

"Don't do that!" a man nearby warned him. "Ravens are bad luck, you know. They say that ravens are a sign of death. If you anger it, death will come for you next."

"That's just an old, stupid superstition," the street urchin said, continuing to wave his hands at me. "You're nothing more than a stupid bird, aren't you?"

My eyes looked like glowing circles in the reflection of the urchin's lantern. I spread my wings wide and started to soar, making sure to swoop nearer to him so that he could feel the powerful rush of air from beneath my wingspan.

"Nevermore!" I called as I flew up into the sky.

"See that?" I heard the older one say as I left them below. "That creature was a demon in bird form."

44

Chapter Four

Iflew through the night sky, feeling both disturbed and at peace. What would I say upon arriving home? Would I fabricate a tale of how the man had found solace or would I tell the truth about his descent into the irretrievable madness that had seen him meet with a violent end? Either way, there was scope to move on now. Before reaching the end of my journey though, I would need to decide what to say.

Sometimes, I thought as I flew, *lies are the best way to forge ahead.*

I had an enlightened and experienced perspective on the moral shades of grey that most ignorant people could not understand. To many, there was simply right or wrong and nothing in between. I knew that was far from the truth. I knew that there were more shades between those two polar opposite ideals. Sometimes lies were the path to truth, sometimes they were the only way to avoid getting bogged down by truths that had been twisted more perversely than any lie could ever be. This was one such occasion. The truth of the matter was that the man had released his desperate hold on his lost love. To move forward, the matter of how he had gone about it would need to be disregarded. Telling of his madness and his destructive end would serve no purpose. With that conclusion, I made my decision.

I had never been human, not exclusively anyway. I wondered what it must feel like to be trapped in such a limiting existence. I wondered why more people didn't end up losing their mind, and how some of them were able to make it to the afterlife relatively unscathed. I imagined it was only a small few that were able to accomplish such a thing.

As I crossed the threshold from the land of the living and back into the afterlife, I felt a huge sense of relief. It wasn't often that I went among the living. I hated having to do it. I had gone more frequently before, when *she* was there. I had only agreed to my most recent visit there in order to set things right, or at least try to.

I flew down through the clouds and brushed the tops of the trees with the tips of my wings. In the distance, I could see my home; a spired, tall castle made of black stone. There were many other buildings nearby that looked the same, and many other ravens too. Some chose to remain in the afterlife, ignoring their gift of being able to traverse between the worlds. Others, more commonly, went back and forth frequently to keep an eye on loved ones left behind – or simply out of curiosity and for amusement. I had done something that none of the other ravens had ever done though. I had fallen in love.

Many of the others shunned me once they found out what I had done. They felt it to be unnatural and chaotic. But, like most things, I had a different viewpoint on the matter and so I let their opinions wash over me as irrelevant. Even in the afterlife there were prejudices. I had neither the time nor the desire to engage with them. There were few things that I enjoyed enough to allow into my time and thoughts. The most important thing to me was *her*.

As I descended upon my castle, I made a narrow turn towards an open window. I flew through it and into a starkly beautiful bedroom. I stretched out my wings and touched my feet down onto the floor. In a transfixed moment, my talons changed into toes and from the toes sprouted the rest of my muscular body. My black feathery wings vanished, leaving behind chiselled arms attached to a bare chest.

Inside my home, I had shed my raven form in exchange for that of a man, another one of my rare gifts. I was not the only raven capable of this but there were not many who possessed the ability. I walked nakedly across the floor of my bedroom and into the open arms of the woman who had been waiting for me. I buried my face in her hair and wrapped my arms around her.

"Lenore," I exclaimed.

"I missed you," she whispered against my cheek. "I feared that something might have been wrong when you were gone for so long."

I pulled my head away from hers and looked at her intently with my black eyes. She stared back at me in return.

"Is there something wrong?" she asked.

I hesitated, wavering for a moment over my commitment to my choice of words.

"No. Nothing is wrong. I am just glad to be home. I don't like going there."

"I know you don't," Lenore said gently. "Thank you for doing it for me."

I stroked her hair with my fingers and leaned forward to softly kiss her lips, my long black hair falling against her as I did.

It had been merely by chance that I'd met Lenore.

She was still among the living then. I had seen her one afternoon as I was sitting on a nearby tree overlooking the open-air market in an older district of the town. She was humming a rather melancholy but beautiful tune. It caught my attention as the sound of it carried to my ears on the breeze. She walked from vendor to vendor buying flowers, fresh breads and cheeses. I was enchanted by her beauty and intrigued by the sad tune that she carried at the tip of her tongue throughout the day. When I followed her home that evening, I sat on the window ledge outside her house and watched her through the glass panes. I saw that she had a man, and that he was one who seemed to adore her. He had been waiting for her and attended to her immediately. He took her parcels to put away and trimmed her freshly cut flowers to put in a glass vase filled with water. He cut and laid out the bread and cheese and poured her a glass of wine. It seemed to me that she was doted on and admired. But still, something caught my attention that made me uneasy; the solemn tune that she continued to hum even late into the night.

I stayed at the house that night, watching from the window even as the man undressed her and laid over her on the floor in front of the fireplace hearth. I watched in sick curiosity as the man had sex with her. Even as the act was being done, my superior senses could still hear the faint hum that escaped her lips. So faint, that the man on top of her wouldn't have been aware of it. I found the whole thing very interesting but I had no plans to linger for more than that one night. Until, that is, she looked at me.

There, on the floor on her back, while the man was inside her, she had turned her head towards the window and had seen me sitting there. She had smiled at me with a smile that was clearly a mask – all to hide the single tear rolling over her cheek. I stayed and stared at her with my black beady bird eyes. I held her gaze until the act was done. The man kissed her and she kissed him back. The two of them then went to bed as if everything was normal and happy.

I didn't leave the ledge of that house for the whole night. I ended up staying there for several days – unless it was to follow her into the markets where I'd sit nearby listening to the soft sound of her humming. It was the longest I had ever been away from the afterlife; I felt uncomfortable and at home with it all at the same time. I became increasingly brazen the longer I watched her.

Once, I had flown right down and landed in front of her feet as she stood looking at a stand full of fresh herbs. To anyone else, all birds would have looked the same. But not to her. She recognised me from outside her window. She reached down to stroke the top of my head. The street vendor, along with several other shoppers, looked aghast at how I had allowed myself to be touched and at how disgusting and unclean it was for her to touch such a wild animal. It was then that our true relationship began.

As my castle in the afterlife remained empty, I stayed in the land of the living for her. During the days, I would sit with her on the open spaces of grass inside the town's quiet park while she fed me crusts of bread and laughed with glee as I pranced about with widespread wings. I would even allow her to hold me and would perch on the side of her hand as she gently rubbed my glossy feathers. At night, I would follow her back to her house at a distance, my black body blending in with the night sky. I didn't actually need to follow in such secrecy; she always knew I was there and each time she and the man would engage in intercourse, she looked to the window to lock eyes with the bird that kept watch over her.

My ability to transform into a man while in the afterlife made me seem even more demonic than most already thought me to be, but I cared not. I was only interested in lingering around Lenore. She had a man though. She seemed committed to him despite how unhappy she looked most of the time. And for as much as I could tell, the man loved her. It wasn't until Lenore's death that I'd started to question everything.

Death was nothing like what most people thought it to be. There was no life afterwards for people who were not already predisposed to the supernatural. There was no glowing light calling souls home to an angelic place in the sky, nor was there any burning pit of flames for the truly evil to suffer eternally within. There was only the end; the complete absence of everything. And that is where most humans would end up: just gone. The same held true for Lenore when she died. The man had her body buried, and her existence was wiped clean from all but his memory.

For a few days I lingered near the house and eavesdropped over people in the town who spoke of her sudden death. Everything I saw and heard seemed to have no clear answer. Lenore's death was unexpected but not suspicious, at least not to anyone in the town. The man acted as any bereaved widower would. He was mournful and isolated. He cried and shook his head and looked for hours at trinkets from the life he and Lenore had shared. There was no indication that he was responsible for her death. In fact, it was more believable to most that *she* would have been the cause of the man's madness and indeed, suicide.

Yet still, something didn't sit right with me and as

much as I tried to retreat back to my castle in the afterlife, I just couldn't let it go. I couldn't let *her* go. So, I did the unthinkable; something that was rarely done and even less frequently condoned. I plucked Lenore from death and brought her with me to the afterlife.

At first, her confusion and disorientation was substantial. She remembered nothing from her previous life except for a few stray memories from childhood. She was suddenly in a beautifully dark castle, with a handsome man who seemed vaguely familiar to her – and yet also very intimidating. She was cold and afraid. I had brought her here, and I knew that responsibility for helping her to adjust rested on me.

I put forth all of my effort into making my home warmer and less daunting for her. As she spent time with me, and saw the gentleness of my spirit, her anxieties began to ease, and her memories slowly began to return. She remembered her past life and the man she had spent it with. She also remembered me, the raven. She didn't, however, remember the days that had led up to her death. This was a common thing. The human mind had a tendency to repress memories that caused unbearable pain. But she remembered the man, and the way that he revered her. It troubled her that he would be affected by her death.

It took some time for her to believe that I was the raven she had spent many an afternoon in the park with. At one point I even had to show her my transformation in order to prove it to her. As soon as her eyes beheld it, and as soon as I had turned back into my form as a man, Lenore declared that she had fallen in love with me.

Chapter Five

I had gone back to the land of the living for one reason alone; because Lenore had asked me to. As the days passed, she made herself at home in my castle. She seemed happier than I had ever seen her before. She woke up each morning with excitement for the new day. When I made love to her, her eyes rested passionately in mine. It was different to the tormented stare I used to see through the windowpane as the man made love to her – if you could even call it *love*.

With me, she was happy, and in turn it filled me with the greatest joy I had ever known. Yet still, something seemed to fade little by little each night. Her love for me didn't diminish. A sense of remorse crept about her like a shadow though. Seeing her struggle troubled me and so one night, I finally had to ask her what was wrong. It was difficult, but she told me.

Lenore was haunted by the guilt of a hidden secret;

she was as much to blame for her unhappiness as the man had been. She explained to me how she had made her commitment to him hastily. They were too quick to live together and to speak of marriage and children. They had fallen into a pretend sense of normalcy and with that, she had feigned happiness. I asked her why she would do such a thing. The only answer she could give was the truth.

"Because I thought that's how things should be done," she said.

I didn't understand. I was perplexed by the small-mindedness of humans and the social constructs they pressured themselves into – like a foot being forced into a shoe that was too small. Whether or not I understood though, the reason remained the same. Lenore felt equally to blame for having entered into an arrangement that didn't fulfil her, and she had tried for years to pretend otherwise. She told me that she was equally to blame for her death but refused to elaborate further on how she'd died, insisting that she couldn't remember the occurrence. All that she could remember was the feeling of remorse. She carried around the guilt of having ruined the man's life by leaving him in death. As happy as she found herself with me, the feeling of grim responsibility wore her down. I knew that she could never truly be free – truly happy – until the man had moved on from her. Now dead, of course the man had moved on, and with him had died all of his mournful connections to Lenore. She was free.

"How was he?" she asked.

I drew my mouth slowly from hers. My still-nude body stood tightly pressed against hers as she ran her fingers down by back. It still amazed her how I could go from having an array of feathers one moment, to a span of soft skin the next.

"He was sad," I answered her honestly. "But he has moved on now and has forgotten about you."

Lenore looked at me in shock and disbelief.

"Really?" she asked.

"Yes, really."

I was telling the truth. In death, the man's memory of Lenore had been extinguished. There was no longer anything to hold on to, for the sake of guilt or otherwise. I didn't feel the need to go into detail about how the man had moved on, only that he had. Her look changed from one of shock to one of great relief. Finally, she could be happy and free of remorse, to love me and our new eternity together. She smiled and ran her hand through my hair. It was as smooth and as glossy as the feathers she had stroked when I was a bird.

"Thank you," she said. "I know it wasn't easy for you to do, or to see. But now that I know he is happy and has let go, I can do the same."

I didn't say anything. I simply kissed her again. She was wearing a black gown made from a shimmering silk woven only in the afterlife from silkworms that lived within the castle's cellars. I unlaced it. The thin garment fell to the ground in silence. I pulled Lenore's body towards mine and then lifted her to carry her to the bed. She wrapped her legs around my waist and trembled in anticipation and excitement as I put her down on the bed and crawled over her.

The sheets on the bed looked like a liquid silver and she felt as though she was wrapped in a dream of pure enticement. In all the times that I had made love to her, and over all the days and nights that we had spent together since I had brought her to the afterlife, it had never crossed her mind to call me by name. She had never felt that she needed a name when she was so sure that she already knew my soul. This time though, as I pushed into her, she felt truly able to freely give herself to me; she wanted to call out my name.

"Tell me your name," she said, breathing heavily.

I hesitated.

"Surely you must have one," she said, smiling with pleasure. "I want to call it out."

A sense of conflict stirred within me. I was yearning to tell her but I was also cautious.

Lenore's mouth began to form a small frown at my apprehension. She was confused about why I would want to keep anything from her. And so I relented and told her my name as a gesture of my deep love for her.

"Rainier," I said.

She grinned and cupped my face in her hands, guiding it down so that I could kiss her. I moved inside of her. We moved with each other until she called my name in satisfaction.

I settled down beside her and pulled the smooth silver sheet over us as she rested her head on my shoulder. She closed her eyes to sleep, completely unaware of the power I had just given her over me.

The next morning when she woke, I was standing at the window that overlooked the land outside of the castle.

"Are you going to fly this morning?" she asked.

She walked up behind me and wrapped her arms

around my waist, folding her hands against my chest and burying her head against my back.

"Not this morning," I answered.

"Is everything ok?"

I usually flew every morning. I would wake, transform into a bird, and take off for an hour or so to survey the lands around my castle, feeling the air pulse beneath my wings. Sometimes I would bring trinkets back for her; wildflowers, gemstones, or randomly interesting bits that I'd found thinking that she might find them beautiful. It was unusual for me not to be keen to spread my wings and fly at the start of the day. Usually while I was gone, she would read in the chair I'd set by the fireplace for her. It was a high-backed, winged chair covered in black velvet with a footstool to match.

I turned around to smile at her reassuringly.

"I am fine," I said. "I would just prefer to stay with you this morning."

My lie was convincing enough. After all, I was adept at lying when it was necessary.

That evening, we made love under the light of a full moon which shone in through the castle window. She again called my name. In the morning when she woke, I was already gone.

When I returned from my flight, I found her elsewhere in the castle, making crusted bread smeared with honey to snack on. She smiled when she saw me walk towards her and asked how my morning flight had been. I sat with her and told her of all the wondrous things I had seen from the skies above. She listened intently to each detail.

"I wish I could fly," she said thoughtfully.

"I wish you could too," I replied.

Had Lenore been more observant, she might have noticed the slight inflection in my voice indicating that I was lying. I loved her deeply, but there were just some things that had to be kept a secret. One such thing was how I had been able to retrieve her from death. Death was not a kind force to reckon with. Even ravens were too fearful of death's presence to deal with it. But I had been blinded by my love for Lenore, and so I felt nothing but hope and longing when I had approached death to ask for permission to take her from the nothingness and bring her to the afterlife.

Death was not one to offer favours or mercies, but it had a modicum of respect for me. Death agreed to release Lenore to me, but there was of course, a condition to be paid. Everything had a balance, even in death.

I offered my castle – and even my service to death – in order to meet the bargain. I had heard that sometimes death used ravens to do its bidding in the land of the living. But none of those things interested death. It was much more curious to see and test the strength of my love for Lenore. It was out of this curiosity that death set the terms for what Lenore's release would cost.

Death would permit me to take Lenore, but in return, should she ever know my name, she would potentially have control over my ability to transform. I was perplexed by this arrangement, but I took it anyway, thinking that even if Lenore *did* end up finding out my name, it wouldn't matter. I loved her and I was certain that she loved me as well. There was nothing to fear if she ended up having control over my ability to change from man to bird or vice versa. I knew that she would never exploit that power over me.

There is a funny thing that happens once your freedom no longer belongs to you. It is a sensation similar to fear, but a thousand times worse. In Lenore asking me my name, the bargain I had made with death suddenly appeared at the front of my mind. I was still certain that Lenore would do nothing to hurt me and that if I had just told her of the cost for her retrieval from death, that she would surely understand and honour my name by never saying it. Still though, there was something gnawing at me and causing an uncertain feeling.

I probably should have made up a name, or refused to give it at all, but that was not the relationship that I wanted with her. I wanted to trust her, I just didn't like the feeling of someone else having control over my form. Not even her.

The way the arrangement worked, was that upon her saying my name, I would remain in whatever form I was in until the next time she said it, freeing me to regain control over my transforming ability. The reason I hadn't taken flight the morning after revealing my name to Lenore, was that I couldn't. It was no longer an option. I couldn't turn into a bird until she said my name again, thus releasing me from being trapped within my human form. The following night, when she'd called my name once more, I was free to change form as I pleased – at least until she said my name again.

And so it would go on each and every time she called me by name. Sometimes it was in the throes of passion, other times it was merely in innocent conversation. I dealt with it as gracefully as I could, sometimes missing my morning flights and concocting excuses of wanting to spend the morning making love. She had never called my name to me while I was in bird form; *that* would be much harder to handle. I figured that I didn't need to worry about that occurrence much though, since most of the time that I spent with her, I did so as a man.

Just like everywhere else, there were whispers in the afterlife; word travelled on the lips of those who should keep to themselves. On one particular morning, while I was off in flight and Lenore sat reading by the fire, another inhabitant of the afterlife came to the castle to pay me a visit. The visitor didn't know me personally, it was only through stories heard that she'd become curious enough to entertain the idea of meeting me, just to see if the rumours were true. The woman seemed pleasant enough and so Lenore invited her inside the castle to wait for my return. In casual conversation, the woman acted as if she had forgotten the name of her old friend the raven, and Lenore was naive enough to tell it to her. As soon as she could hear my beating wings, the woman raced to the window and called my name at me while I remained in bird form.

I flew inside the room and immediately set my foot down on the floor as a man. I stood nakedly before both women, fury burning throughout my whole being. The word didn't work on the lips of the stranger, for the agreement with death linked the curse to Lenore's voice only. Upon seeing this, the stranger fled the castle, but not before the damage had been done. Lenore had seen my outrage and although she tried to calm me with a gentle caress of her hand, I brushed her aside in anger.

"What made you think you could tell that woman my name?!" I shouted at her.

She had never seen me so angry before and took steps backwards.

"She said she was an old friend of yours," Lenore replied anxiously. "I'm sorry, I didn't know."

I could see that I had scared her, and I knew that it wasn't her fault. After all, if I had only told her what the consequences would be of my name being poured from her lips, she would have known better. I couldn't complain of her ignorance when it was through no fault of her own. I approached her slowly and reached for her hand. I rested my head against hers and sighed.

"I'm sorry," I said. "I didn't mean to get angry with you."

"It's ok," she answered, relieved that the moment had passed. "But I don't understand why you are so touchy about your name. What did that woman want with you anyway?"

"I don't know."

Lenore was left with a lingering feeling that I did know, despite what I'd told her.

Chapter Six

Time passed in happiness for Lenore and I. We didn't give any more thought back to the day of our unwanted visitor. Despite this, Lenore seemed to watch me more closely than she had before. Unless it was during a moment of unbridled passion in which she wasn't thinking, she didn't call my name as often. I was glad for it because it meant no more missed mornings of flight and no more awkwardness whilst waiting to hear my name said again in order for my freedom of form to be reinstated.

One night as I held her in my arms by the fire, Lenore asked me a question.

"Are there others like you?"

"Other ravens?"

"Yes," she confirmed. "Other ravens who can turn into men?"

"Yes, a few."

"So it is uncommon then?"

"Yes."

"Do they have names too?"

She was trying to make her question sound as innocent as possible.

"Why do you ask me this?"

"I ask only out of simple curiosity."

"Yes," I answered, holding her close against my chest. "They have names as well. Everyone has a name."

"I suppose that is true," Lenore mused.

"What was the name of the man at your house?" I asked.

She had not expected that question. Having felt freed from him, she hadn't thought about him since the day I'd told her that he'd moved on.

"Edgar," she answered plainly.

And just like that, the conversation ended.

That night in bed, Lenore dreamt that she was standing at the window watching me fly towards her. In the dream, she called out my name, and as she did, I immediately turned into a man and fell to my death on the rocks below. She awoke in a frightened sweat. In search of comfort she frantically pulled herself closer to me.

"Are you alright?" I asked as I woke.

I had felt her quivering against me. She had a troubled look in her eyes.

"Yes," she lied. "I'm fine. I just had a nightmare."

"What was it about?"

"I can't remember."

Another lie.

There are few things as damaging to a relationship as secrets and lies, and yet, lovers seem to have trouble keeping away from them.

Once the morning arrived, I kissed Lenore gently on the cheek. She went to the window and watched me fly away. She stayed there the entire time I was gone. When she saw me flying back towards her, she broke into a cold sweat, deep in thought about her dream.

As I got closer to the window, Lenore took steps backwards to let me inside the room. She was convinced that her dream meant nothing at all and wasn't even sure why she was entertaining the idea that it was anything other than her imagination at play. Yet still, she couldn't bring herself to chance the possibility of me getting hurt. As soon as I was about to change back into a man, she spoke my name, keen to test the power of the word.

"Rainier," she said in a matter-of-fact tone.

I stared at her in shock as I opened my wingspan, which by now would have turned into the same arms that held her each night. They remained nothing more than feathers and bone. I landed on the floor in front of her feet and looked up at her through glassy onyx eyes. Lenore knelt down and looked at me in confusion.

"Why haven't you changed back into a man?" she asked.

I said nothing. We both stared at each other in fear and uncertainty while Lenore pondered what had happened. She reached out her hand and I hopped onto it. She lifted me and gently set me in her lap.

"Rainier," she said as tears welled in her eyes. "Why are you still a bird?"

With the utterance of my name once more, I stepped off from her lap and changed myself back into a man. There was no more hiding; I now had to tell Lenore about the deal I had made with death.

She listened to me tell the story until I was done. At times, she cried over what I had sacrificed in order to save her from death and bring her to me here in the afterlife. At other times, she squeezed my hand in hers, in awe of how much she loved me, and I her.

"Why didn't you tell me of this before now?" she asked. "All of this time, I could have known, and you would not have suffered so."

"I haven't suffered," I smiled. "Missing a flight here and there was no hardship when instead, that time was spent with you."

"I don't want there to be any more secrets between us," she said. "Promise me."

I didn't want there to be secrets between us either. I was content to agree. In my haste to trust and love – and in my desire to be trusted and loved in return – I was too eager to overlook the fact that I still had one big secret hidden from Lenore; the one about how Edgar had died. It was too late though. By the time I had agreed to my promise and had realised that I still had something to hide, the opportunity had passed.

Edgar was gone and there was no returning from death for him, so it was an easy secret to forget about. At least until the day when Lenore asked if she could visit the land of the living!

"Why would you want to go there?" I asked.

Ever since learning of the curse that held my name, she had been extremely careful to only say it during moments of love, in which she could immediately say it soon after, thereby not holding any power over my ability to transform for more than a mere second or two.

"I'd just like to see what it looks like in my absence."

Suddenly, I knew that the secret I had been holding on to was likely to cause harm.

"Is it impossible for me to go and see for myself what my old world looks like now, since I am not a raven like you?" she asked.

There was no malice to her intent. She simply wanted to revisit her old home; a mere nostalgic indulgence with me by her side.

Even though I had kept the secret of Edgar's death, I was devoted to not breaking any more trust with Lenore. I could not lie to her after having made that promise, not even about this.

"Yes, it is possible for you to see into the land of the living through my eyes. You do not have the ability to go there yourself though."

"Through your eyes? How would I do that?"

"There is a special tea, one that would allow you to see what I can when I fly into the world of the living. The effect doesn't last for long – maybe several hours at most."

"I would like to try it," she said.

"I don't think that's a good idea. I don't think any good would come of it. Are you not happy here with me?"

"Of course I am. I am happier than I can ever remember being. But it does trouble me sometimes that I cannot remember how I died. Does it not trouble you?"

"No. It matters not how you died. It only matters that you are here now, with me."

She ran her fingers through my hair and pressed her forehead against mine. It was one of our most intimate gestures; it reminded Lenore of how affixed she used to be on my raven eyes through the glass windowpanes of Edgar's house.

"Perhaps if I could just see the house again, it might jog my memory and help me to know what happened."

The house, I thought. *The house burned to the ground and is no longer there.*

"Are you sure you even want to know the answers?" I asked. "Do you not remember how unhappy you were when I first saw you there?"

"I do," she answered. "And you saved me both from that, and from death. And now I am asking you to save me once more."

"Save you from what?"

"From the consuming longing to know what happened. I feel as though I need to put my questions to rest once and for all. You helped me to rest my unease about Edgar. Now I need you to help me rest my unease about what happened to me. Please," she begged.

"What if there are no answers to be found? What if looking back there doesn't help you to remember anything at all?"

"Then at least I can take comfort in the knowledge that I tried to seek answers."

"And that will be enough for you?" I asked.

"Yes."

That evening, I brewed the special tea that would grant Lenore the gift of vision through my eyes.

When we went to bed that night, there was a sense of restlessness blanketing us both. I wanted to get it over with; perhaps in seeing that the house was no more, it would be the end of Lenore's search for answers. Perhaps that alone would provide some closure. After all, any number of things could have caused the house to burn down. The ashes wouldn't prove that Edgar had burned with it. The chances of Lenore jumping to that conclusion were slim. It was more likely that she would think he had moved on and that the house fire had happened thereafter.

Lenore's night was an uncomfortable one. Her thoughts swayed between moments of bliss and moments of concern, a trait that might have caused me to be worried if I had given it more attention.

The next morning, once Lenore had finished her cup of tea and sat down in her chair, I set off in flight to the land of the living – something I hadn't expected or intended on doing again.

The tea worked in an omnipresent manner. Lenore and I could see our own surroundings, but she could also see mine. She sat against her dark velvet chair as her eyes clouded over. She could see what it was like to fly through the sky as a raven. Sight was the only thing that the tea allowed her to share though. We could not exchange thoughts, voices, or feelings. And the gift only worked in one direction; she could see what I could, but I could not see what she could.

I flew purposefully. I didn't wish to be among the living for long. I had only promised Lenore that I would circle through the town and once around her old house. Straight after that, I would head back to the afterlife.

When I got to the town, I did as I had promised. I circled the house quickly but efficiently. I did not wish to have to do this again.

From her chair, Lenore saw the town that she recognised as her old home. She saw the market that she loved to walk through and the park where she used to sit with me. Through my eyes, she witnessed my flight towards the empty space where her house used to stand. As I circled the patch of land, there was still rubble on the ground even after all this time. The townsfolk were obviously not in any hurry to tend to it. It had deteriorated into the ground. Weeds were growing up in between the remains.

I could see that there was nothing identifiable or remarkable left. But Lenore saw the scene differently. Her memory filled in the missing pieces of visual information, and somehow reached the conclusion of the atrocities committed. She felt as if she couldn't breathe, as if her lungs were being filled and suffocated with smoke. She felt as if the heat from the hearth in front of her chair was choking her, even though there was no fire. She wanted to end the sight that she was sharing with me, but she wasn't able to. I hadn't told her how to snap out of it, or even if there was a way to end the effect of the tea before it wore off.

As I flew swiftly home, hoping to find the matter resolved, Lenore sat panicked in her chair until she passed out.

When her eyes opened, she found herself being held in my arms. I had a cool cloth against her brow and had loosened the lace-up ties on her gown.

"What happened?" she asked.

She looked up at me. Her head was pounding and her hands were shaking.

"Sometimes sharing sight can be a bit overwhelming," I said. "I should have warned you about that. When I got back, I found you unconscious in your chair. I think you must have passed out. But you're alright now and I am here."

She snuggled against me, thankful that I was home and that the ghastly vision was over.

"Did you get the answers you were looking for?" I asked.

"No. Do you know what happened to that house?"

I quickly tried to come up with an answer that wouldn't be a lie. Lenore's head was already pressed against my chest and she heard my heart start to race.

"Why does that question make you nervous?" she asked. "Is there something you have been keeping from me?"

I couldn't bring myself to tell her more lies. I knew that the truth would upset her, maybe even anger her, but perhaps if she knew what had actually happened then her search for answers would cease.

"Yes."

Now it was turn for her heart to race.

"I am sorry, my love. I didn't mean to keep this from you, but I feared it would upset you too much to know. I had hoped that you would find enough peace here with me to question it no further, but I can see that you will not be satisfied until you know the truth. So I will tell you, and then you must promise me to move on from this so that it can finally be over."

Lenore was disappointed and saddened that I had kept more secrets from her. Still though, she hadn't lost confidence that it had been done in order to protect her and with good reason. With this in mind, she agreed to hear whatever it was, and then move on.

I told her of my time at the house with Edgar. I told her everything that I remembered, including the angst and insufferable sorrow, leaving out only the part about Edgar masturbating to her portrait. I told her how I had tried to help, but that the man was unreachable in his despair and that his slow descent from sanity to madness was unavoidable. Finally, I told her about Edgar's death and how he had burned the house down around him in the hope of being reunited with her in the afterlife. I wanted her to find peace in the fact that nothing that had happened was her fault, and that Edgar loved her even until his dying moment. I was hopeful that this would satisfy every question that she had, and that finally, after all this time, we could be free to live happily forever.

Lenore sat quietly for a while until the moment became uncomfortably silent. When she did speak, it was not a question that I had expected to hear.

"Why did you rescue me from death?" she asked.

I shook my head. I found it odd that she would even wonder.

"Because I love you. Surely you already knew

that?"

"I did," she said. "I am just trying to wrap my mind around the fact that whilst one man entered death to have me, another plucked me from it for the very same reason."

I had never really thought about it like that, although logistically I supposed it was true.

"Is it possible to remove *anyone* from death?" she asked.

"I don't know. Why?"

"I'm just curious." Lenore shifted her position in my lap. "So you had never brought someone out of death before me?"

"No. Only you."

"And you are one of the only few that can do it I assume?"

"Yes. Lenore, what is the point of the questions that you're asking?"

"I am just curious," she said. "I'm really tired now though. Can we go to bed?"

"Yes," I said. "Are we finished with all of this now?"

"Yes. I think we are."

I carried her in my arms towards the bed where we snuggled down next to each other.

For several days, there was no mention of what had happened. Lenore seemed more at ease and more content than she had been for a while. I was happy that things were back to normal and had all but forgotten my worries about the curse over my name. It seemed that there were no longer any secrets between us – just love and the happiness of being together.

Ravens were always fabled to be one of the smartest birds. Perhaps if I had not been so blinded by my feelings for Lenore, I would have managed to live up to that reputation.

Chapter Seven

During one of my morning flights, Lenore ventured out of the castle and went for a walk in the woods alone. Once into the depths of the tall trees, she could hear footsteps following behind her. Feeling a little afraid, she bravely turned around. Stood before her was the stranger who had paid her a visit at the castle.

"What are you doing out here alone in the woods?" the woman asked Lenore.

"I could ask you the same thing."

The woman said nothing.

"To be honest," Lenore continued. "I was hoping that I might find you. Or that you would find me."

"Why?"

The woman looked entirely confused as to why Lenore would want to have anything to do with her after what had happened at the castle.

"Do you know how to find death?" Lenore asked.

"That's a rather strange question to ask," the woman replied, surprised and intrigued.

"Yes," Lenore continued. "I seem to be full of strange questions, I guess. Well, do you?"

"I do," said the woman.

"I thought so. Can you take me to speak with death?"

"Why would you want to do that? And why would you ask me? You have one of the most powerful ravens in the afterlife at your beck and call."

Lenore was slightly caught off guard at the mention of me.

"Oh, I see," the woman said, grinning widely. "You don't want him to know."

Lenore winced in discomfort.

"Why not?" asked the woman. "Your lover is probably more familiar in dealing with death than any of us are. He was able to coax death into giving you up. Not many can bargain with death."

"From what I understand, death didn't exactly *give*

anything," said Lenore. "There was a deal made, which I can tell you are already aware of. Why else would you try to call the raven's name to see if that power worked?"

"Does it work?"

"Only for me."

"I can take you to see death, but I want something in return."

"What do you want?"

Lenore wasn't even sure how much she actually wanted to pay a visit to death yet. She had no idea how much such a visit would be worth.

"I want a night with your lover," said the woman.

"For what purpose?" Lenore asked in shock.

"Oh, I think you can guess what I have in mind. You have looked at him, right? He is one of the most gorgeous men in the afterlife."

"No!" Lenore insisted. "I'm not agreeing to that. Forget it."

A sick feeling bubbled in Lenore's stomach. Confused and defensive, she started to walk away.

"Wait," the woman called after her. "There might

be something else I want instead."

Lenore turned slowly on her heels to listen to the woman's proposition.

"Well then, what is it? What do you want?" Lenore asked.

A shade of malevolence fell over the woman's face.

"I want to know what death says to you," she said.

"I don't see how that would benefit you in the slightest," replied Lenore. "Why would a conversation about matters that don't concern you be of interest?"

The woman looked as though she was trying too hard to appear innocent.

"Let's just say I'm curious," she said.

"Fine," Lenore agreed. "I'll tell you what death says."

The woman extended her hand out for Lenore to shake. As soon as Lenore made contact though, the woman dug a nail into the side of her wrist.

"Oww! What was that for?!" Lenore shouted.

"That was to make sure you keep your end of the bargain. You've just agreed in blood. In the afterlife, when you make a promise in blood, it's as good as selling your soul. If you don't tell me what death says to you, or if you try to make something up, you'll die."

"I'm already dead," said Lenore, laughing anxiously.

"No, what I mean is that you will be returned to death. Your raven won't be able to get you back out this time. It would be unwise of you to break our agreement."

Lenore felt a chill go up her spine. She wasn't even sure why she was doing this anymore, or what had possessed her to agree to this woman who had already tried to kill me by using my name against me mid-flight.

"Fine. Take me to death now."

"I can't," said the woman.

"What? But we just agreed. You just said…"

"I can't take you *right now*," the woman interrupted. "Death doesn't like to be disturbed in the early morning. I can take you at the witching hour tonight."

Lenore thought about how she could sneak out from under my arms during our sleep to run off in the middle of the night to seek out death. The very notion of deceiving me filled her with dread and guilt. But she had to ask death a vital question and this was the only way to do it. She knew that I wouldn't understand, not this time.

"Where shall I meet you?"

"Right here is fine," said the woman. "See you tonight!"

Lenore didn't trust the woman. She was starting to wonder whether she could even trust herself.

That evening, as I slept soundly in our bed, Lenore slid silently out from under my arms, quietly got dressed, and went out to meet the woman under the cover of darkness. The woman was already there, just as she'd said she would be. Silently, she motioned for Lenore to follow her. They walked deeper into the woods. When they came to the opening of a cave, the woman pointed inside.

"You'll find death in there," she said.

She handed Lenore the lantern that she had been carrying.

"How can I be sure that I can trust you?" Lenore asked.

"You can't."

Fair enough, Lenore thought to herself. The woman was right; nothing could be done to prove whether or not she could be trusted. Lenore turned and walked into the mouth of the cave realising that this shady choice might just be her last.

The cave was damp and was scented with moist mildew and rotten leaves. Lenore walked for what felt like too long, until suddenly, she saw a shadow move off in the distance.

"Hello?" she called into the cave.

The voice that answered her was nothing like what she'd expected death to sound like. If choking on silence could be a sound, *that* was what the voice sounded like. It was a small and twisted utterance, but the inflection of it was so distorted that it seemed to ring loudly in Lenore's head despite its low volume.

"Come no closer," it said. "What do you want?"

"Are you death?" Lenore asked.

She had stopped walking and was affixed to her spot.

"I am."

"I have a question to ask you."

"I know."

"How can you know what the question is before I have even asked it?"

"You want to know if I have Edgar," it answered.

Lenore felt immediately nauseous.

"Yes," she said timidly. "I do."

"I have him."

Lenore was shocked and didn't know what to say.

"That answer was not enough for you my dear, was it? You want to know if you can take him from me."

Lenore ignored the burning in her throat and spoke anyway.

"Is there a way for Edgar to come into the afterlife?" she asked.

"Why would you want that? Are you not happy with your raven?"

"Oh yes, I am very happy with Rainier."

"Then you do not ask because you *want* to release Edgar; you ask because you are afraid that he might get out. Am I correct?"

Death's words stung Lenore like venomous bites.

"Yes."

"You have nothing to worry about my dear," death taunted. "The only one here that would be able to pull Edgar into the afterlife, is your raven. And I doubt he would want to do such a thing – he is in love with you. Besides, every release from death must be paid for, and your raven has nothing more to give that I desire. I have no use for castles or beautiful things."

Lenore was relieved. She didn't know whether or not she should thank death for the answers. She figured that the best thing to do was just to get out of the cave and leave death in peace.

When she saw the woman still waiting for her at the mouth of the cave, Lenore was ready to hurry back to me. There was still the agreement to be honoured though.

"What did it say?" asked the woman.

Lenore stared at her with a blank expression.

"What did death say to you?" the woman repeated. "Don't tell me you're going to break your promise. If you do, you might as well go back in the cave and hand yourself over to death."

Lenore had no choice but to answer the woman honestly.

"Death told me that there is no way into the afterlife for a man I once knew – unless the raven should wish to make a deal to get him in. My lover has no desire to do that, and death said there is nothing it wants from the raven anyway. The matter is therefore closed. I am happy to accept that."

The two started to head back to the castle. For most of the time, they walked in silence. But then the woman thought of something else that she wanted to know.

"You are clearly desperate for the man you knew to be kept out of the afterlife. He must have done something quite horrible."

Lenore stayed quiet and kept walking.

"What was it? What did he do that makes you so anxious to avoid him forever?"

"I have already answered the question that I owed you. I do not need to tell you anything else."

The woman shrugged and a grin crawled across her face. She pointed up at the castle, towards me.

"You might want to tell *him* though," she said.

I was standing in front of the entrance gate. I had stirred and had noticed Lenore's absence.

She was nervous about how she would explain her nighttime venture and she was anxious that I would probably be furious with her for seeking out death – and for going behind my back to have dealings with the strange woman. Feeling relieved about death's answer though, Lenore was happy to see me. She walked up to me and wrapped her arms around me. The other woman waved at me teasingly and then left.

"Where were you?" I asked.

There was a slight edge of anger to my voice, but it was mostly softened by relief. When I had realised that Lenore was missing, I had feared the worst, even though I didn't know what the worst could possibly be.

"Let's go inside to talk about it," she answered.

Chapter Eight

"Why would you do such a thing!?" I asked, exasperated.

I was visibly upset after hearing Lenore's account of where she had gone in the middle of the night and why.

"If you are still in love with that man and are that desperate to have him back, you should have just told me," I said. "My heart would be in pieces, but I would bring him here if that's what you want. I love you, Lenore. Can't you see that I am at your mercy?"

"No!" Lenore wailed.

She looked at me with tears in her eyes, feeling the pang of remorse for having caused me to question her love. She reached to grab my hands, pulling me closer to her.

"That is not it at all! I do not love Edgar. I did at one time, or at least I thought I did. Whatever it was, it died out a long time ago."

"I don't understand," I said.

I sat down on the velvet chair, Lenore's hands still in mine. She got down on her knees before me and tried to explain.

"All this time, I've just needed to know that I'll never have to see Edgar again. That's why I wanted to see my old home and it's why I went to speak to death. Seeing the burned ash of the house through your eyes reminded me of how I died. It was an accident but all the same, Edgar caused it. He was a madman long before his grief and long before your visit to him. My walks to the market – to see you – were the only moments in which I felt free. Edgar sensed my desire to be away from him and it made him afraid, I think. He feared that one day I wouldn't come back home from the market at all. In an irrational attempt to prove his love to me and make me stay, he ended up causing the accident that resulted in my death. One night after you had watched us through the window, I went into the bedroom with him. Just as I was about to get into our bed, he held me – so tightly that I couldn't breathe. At first, I tried to tell him he was hurting me. His arms were crushing my rib cage and I couldn't fill my lungs with air. The more I tried to talk, the more he hushed me and told me that he loved me. His grip became tighter. He told me that he would never let me go and that one day I would see the strength of his love for me. I don't truly think he meant to hurt me. He was out of his mind with fear that I would leave him. I stood there, unable to breathe. Tears ran down my face as I thought of you sitting just outside the window, close enough to hear me if only I could have made a sound. When Edgar heard my rib cage crack, I think it must have snapped him out of his frenzy and he let me go. It was too late by then."

A horrible feeling washed over me. I left my chair and got down on my knees to be next to Lenore. I gently drew her into me and she rested her head on my shoulder. It hurt me to think that I had been there, helplessly unaware, whilst she had suffered.

"My love," I said. "I am so sorry."

Lenore lifted her head and looked at me, her cheekbones wet with tears.

"It's not your fault," she said. "This is why I have been so troubled and so consumed with making sure that Edgar can never get hold of me again. He was a troubled man. I was afraid of him then and I would be afraid of him now."

I put my hand against Lenore's cheek and wiped

away her tears with my fingertips.

"You have no reason to worry about Edgar ever again," I said. "He is gone forever and can never touch you here. You are safe with me, always."

I put my mouth on hers and we shared a kiss that melted our souls together.

"Then I shall be happy always," Lenore said.

For the first time, she felt completely at peace.

***

Death had been bothered once already that night, so when the woman who had shown Lenore the way to the cave went back there, it was not pleased. Still, when someone ventured to that place there was usually a reason. Death enjoyed capitalising on the selfish reasoning of others.

"What brings you here again?" death asked the woman.

"I have a question," she replied. "I want to know what it is that you might want from the raven."

Death and I had always had a rather respectful relationship. Neither of us wished to interfere with each other.

"The raven?" said death. "What could I possibly

want from the raven?"

"He is powerful, and special, and you seemed interested enough in helping him bring his lover to the afterlife."

"That is because he gave me something in return."

"Yes, I'm aware of your agreement with him. He paid with his name and with the control of his ability to transform – all in order to have *her* here with him. I doubt that you got much in return though. I'm going to guess that you aren't interested in the things that most are; you are attracted to power over others. Am I right to assume that?" the woman asked.

"I enjoy being one of the most powerful forces known to man, if that is what you mean?"

"But the raven," the woman continued. "He seems very powerful too."

"His power is nothing compared to mine," death announced, louder than before.

"Perhaps," said the woman. "But one could argue that he has a certain power that you do not."

"What power do you think the raven could possibly have that I do not?" death replied, sounding almost amused.

"He holds the power of love over Lenore. He holds the power of transformation in his own will again, now that she refuses to use it against him. He even holds power over you; he cheated you out of a death well-earned and conned you into letting him pluck her from right underneath you. Even Lenore said that you told her the raven is the only one who can bring someone into the afterlife. I was surprised to hear that not even you yourself could do that."

The woman wanted to anger death. There was no truth in her words. I had no quarrel with death and did not seek to hold any power over it. The woman had a spiteful idea – one that would cause chaos and calamity. And all because she couldn't have me for herself.

"It seems to me that there *is* still one thing that you would want from the raven: *his life*," she said.

There was a dark silence in the cave for a few moments as death considered what had been said. There were rules to follow, and death couldn't just take a raven's life without reason. If there was reason though, the act would be legitimately binding. It angered death to think its power had limits – limits that a raven was not bound by.

"Perhaps we could help each other, you and I," death hissed.

"Oh?" the woman said, feigning ignorance.

"How would you like to live in the raven's castle, to have all of his pretty things, and to gratify your scorned and vengeful heart by seeing his love spend her days in misery for as long as she remains here in the afterlife?"

"That sounds delightful."

"Then make Lenore say his name. Make her speak his name while he is in bird form and then snap his neck. The end of the raven's life will mean that his power will cease to exist, and I will reign superior over all things – as should be. You can stay in his castle and enjoy all that was once his."

"And what of Lenore?" the woman asked.

"In exchange for the death of the raven, I will send Lenore something special; something that will promise her a miserable and dark end to her tale of love."

"As tempting as this all sounds, how can I make her speak his name? She knows the power it holds over him and she has vowed never to exploit it. Getting her to call his name whilst he is in bird form would prove to be almost impossible."

"That is none of my concern. I've made you an offer. Take it or leave it."

The woman's desire to harm Lenore and I was greater than her logic. It was on this basis that she agreed and then left death to go and formulate her plan. Surely, she could find some reason to get herself invited inside the castle while I was out on one of my morning flights. If the woman could time it just right, she could reach out and grab me as a bird upon my return through the window. The most difficult part would be in how to get Lenore to call my name. The woman started to think about all of the times one might call out their lover's name; in passion, in anger… *in fear*.

Perfect, she thought.

***

After a night of delicious bliss and intertwined bodies, Lenore and I woke up holding each other. The afterlife was now our perfect place of sanctuary; no threats, no secrets, no time restraints.

We enjoyed a delicious cup of coffee that I'd made and brought into the bed so that we could drink it naked together beneath the blankets as the cool air flowed through the open window.

"I want to make a list of a million wonderful things that we will do together," Lenore said.

"Only a million?" I said jokingly. "Time is very much on our side. Why not several million?"

"I don't think I could write several million at once," Lenore said happily.

"Ok, then begin writing your first of the million this morning while I am out on my flight. When I get back, we will start with number one."

"I love that idea so much," she said.

"And I love you," I replied.

Once we had finished our coffee and playful conversation, I set my cup down on the table near the bed. Lenore got up and pushed her arms through a satin robe as she walked to the window. She kissed me and then I transformed into a bird, ready to take flight. Throughout this, the smile on my face remained.

"I'll be back soon," I said. "I'm looking forward to getting started on our list."

Lenore watched me fly until she could no longer see my black silhouette in the sky. Then, she pulled a paper journal and quill from the nearby table and sat in her chair to write.

Chapter Nine

Lenore was just beginning to write the seventy-ninth item on her list when there was a knock on the castle door that echoed throughout the hall. She set her journal and ink down and went to see who it was.

Standing at the door was the woman.

"Why are you here?" Lenore asked.

"Excuse my intrusion, but I need to talk to you."

"About what?"

"Please, may I come inside?"

"Not until you tell me what this is about," Lenore insisted.

"Death."

Lenore still didn't trust the woman but in a state of panic, she invited her inside.

It was not enough for the woman. She needed to be in the same spot to which I would return. Otherwise, her plan would fail.

"I think the raven will want to hear of this too," the woman said with a sense of urgency. "The matter cannot wait."

Lenore foolishly led the woman to our room. She pulled another chair beside hers so that they could wait together for my return. Lenore considered it to be harmless; she had already told me everything and the woman had no power to use my name against me. The woman looked visibly shaken. Whatever it was she had come to tell us, Lenore was certain it would require my guidance – especially if it had something to do with death. After a few minutes of sitting in awkward silence though, Lenore's curiosity got the better of her.

"Did you go back to speak with death?" she asked.

"Yes," replied the woman. "And oh, how I wish I hadn't."

"Why? What did death say? Why did you go back?"

Lenore's voice was nervous and shaking. It was perfect for the woman's plan.

"I needed to know that you hadn't lied to me," the

woman continued. "I found it strange to think that *your* raven – and not any other single raven in the afterlife – was the only one capable of freeing someone from death."

"He is special," Lenore said defiantly. "He has abilities that others do not."

"True, but it still seems odd that he would be the *only* one."

"But that is what death told me."

"He lied."

The colour drained from Lenore's face as she felt her heart drop into the pit of her stomach.

"What?" she whispered in quiet fear.

"Death lied to you," the woman repeated.

"That's impossible."

"You don't think death is capable of lying?" the woman mocked. "You have an unrealistically high opinion of something that ends lives and traps them in nothingness forever."

"Why would it lie to me?"

The woman thought quickly to come up with a convincing answer.

"Because it can," she insisted. "And because it wants to protect itself from the raven's wrath. The raven will be livid when he finds out what death has done."

Lenore was almost too terrified to speak. The words left her lips like individual drops of poison, each one stinging her as if it were her last.

"What did death do?"

"I'm not sure if I should tell you that yet."

"Please!"

Lenore was almost hysterical. She needed me back from my flight and beside her to calm her trembling nerves.

"Death released Edgar," the woman said plainly.

She was fascinated by the horrified look in Lenore's eyes. Lenore clasped her hand over her mouth to keep herself from screaming – she was definitely in a state of fear now.

"I don't believe you," Lenore murmured. "What reason would death have to do such a thing?"

The woman shrugged her shoulders.

"How should I know?" she said nonchalantly. "I'm not death."

The timing of what happened next was a matter of sheer luck. As I came into view of the window, both Lenore and the woman could see my dark shape flying towards the castle. The woman stood up and walked to the side of the window, nearly out of view from me as I approached. Lenore saw me and stood too. As she walked towards the window to tell me immediately of the awful news she had just heard, she was too upset and too desperate for my help to think clearly about what she was doing. She called out as she rushed up to my approaching shadow.

"Rainier!"

With Lenore too frantic to react in time, the woman reached out her hand and grabbed me as soon as my winged form came through the opening. With her fingers grasped tightly around my throat and a look of sheer panic coming from my dark eyes as I desperately searched my field of vision for Lenore, the woman snapped my neck.

"No!" Lenore screamed.

She ran towards the woman and knocked her to the ground. My lifeless body hit the cold stone floor.

"What have you done?" Lenore screamed at the woman.

Picking up my body, Lenore cradled it against her

chest.

"Rainier," she sobbed. "Rainier, change back! Please!"

"It's too late," the woman sneered. "He's a dead bird, nothing more."

Lenore clenched my lifeless body.

"Why would you do this to us?"

"Why not," the woman answered.

Lenore was blinded by fury and pain. She stood up and ran towards the door of the castle. She couldn't understand why the woman had been so cruel.

"Where are you going?" the woman called after her. "I'm going to steal this castle from you now."

Lenore whipped around to glare at her with all the hatred she could muster amidst her sorrow.

"I don't want this castle," Lenore said in disgust. "Do you think this building even matters to me at all? The only thing that matters to me is in my hands. I am going to speak with death and undo what you have done. Then, once Rainier is restored, we will come back to deal with you."

"Good luck with that," the woman said sarcastically.

She snorted with satisfaction over her deed and sat down in Lenore's velvet chair.

Lenore ran out of the castle. Her feet were bare and her naked body was half-visible beneath the shimmering silk gown she had put on just before I had left for my flight. She tried desperately to remember where death's cave was. She paid no attention to the rocks cutting her feet as she ran, or to the tree branches tearing at her robe as she made her way through the woods.

After several wrong paths, she could finally see the cave. The entire time she had been running, she'd held my limp body against her, cradling my head on her breast. The body was still warm. Once she reached the cave's entrance, she did not hesitate to run straight inside, calling death's name as if seeking a confrontation.

"Death!" she shouted into the blackness of the cave. "Meet me! For I know what you have done, and I am here to seek payment for your misdeed."

"*Misdeed?*" death answered.

Lenore couldn't see death. She could only hear its twisted voice as it crept up every wall of the cave around her.

"I know that you released Edgar and brought his presence into the afterlife. I am here to seek payment for what you have done without cause."

Death laughed and then hissed.

"Is *that* what *she* told you? I have done no such thing. But it is an entertaining game that is being played."

"What game?" Lenore asked.

She was angry and confused. She looked around the cave, straining to see where death was hiding in the dark.

"The woman that called on you this morning – did she tell you of this deed?"

"Yes, and it is abhorrent that you would do such a thing after our last meeting."

"As I have said," death repeated. "I did not release Edgar. He remains fully and motionlessly dead."

"What? But then why…"

"You have been outmatched. The woman holds victory over you. She has used your raven as a pawn."

"Why would she do this?"

Death ignored Lenore's question, even though the answer was clear. The woman had done as she'd promised. She had prompted my death, and in turn, Lenore had brought my corpse to the cave. All was going exactly as death had planned. The woman had been rewarded with the castle and everything within its walls. Death had been rewarded with a dead raven – one that would no longer be a threat to its ego. And Lenore would be rewarded with… well, something special; something wickedly and horrifically special.

"What is that you hold in your hands?" death asked, knowing full well it was my corpse.

Lenore was desperate. She had believed the woman and had come to the cave in the hope of persuading death to restore my life. She had nothing to bargain with though. Death hadn't set Edgar free and she had no leverage over death to wield. She was at death's mercy to beg for her lover to be restored. Unfortunately, that was not at all what death had in mind.

Lenore cried as she held my dead body up into the air.

"Please bring Rainier back to the afterlife with me. I will do anything you ask. I will give you anything you want."

Death chuckled. The sound vibrated the ground inside of the cave.

"I do not ask anything of you, nor do I want anything from you."

Before Lenore could react, death snatched my corpse from her hands.

"No!" she screamed. "Give him back to me!"

There was no acknowledgement from death as Lenore screamed into the cave and ran through each tunnel and alcove searching for me and banging her fists against the rock walls. After she had all but nearly exhausted herself, death finally spoke.

"I *will* return something to you," it said.

Lenore paused and wiped her face with the back of her hand to mop up some of the tears. She waited hopefully to hear death say that it would return her raven to her in the afterlife. Regardless of what it may cost, she would pay anything to have me back by her side.

"Go back to the castle and wait there. He will come to you shortly."

Lenore's heart was overjoyed with gratitude.

"Thank you!" she spluttered. "Whatever your price, I will pay it."

Death remained silent.

"What of the woman in our castle?" Lenore asked, suddenly remembering that the woman had taken over our residence.

"Do what you want with her," death answered. "It matters not to me."

At those words, Lenore ran from the cave, keen to get back to the castle to wait for me. She was full of fury for the woman and was not at all opposed to bringing her to a violent end.

When Lenore entered the castle, she did so silently, staying close to the shadows and corners. She could see the woman sitting in her chair, snoring lightly as she slept in front of the roaring fire in the hearth.

Lenore went to the kitchen and pulled a sharp knife from one of the drawers. She had never killed anyone before but she had never wanted to kill anyone as much as she wanted to kill the woman.

The woman's death was quick and to-the-point. Lenore thrust the knife into her throat as she slept. All that could be heard was a slight gurgle as the woman tried to take a breath, instead choking on her own blood. Lenore stood and watched until the woman stopped breathing and her heart stopped beating entirely. Then, she pulled the woman's body from the chair, pushed it to the side on the floor with her feet, and took her place upon her velvet seat again. She stared into the crackling fire and waited for death to make good on its promise and return her raven to her.

Because she hadn't thought to ask how long it would take, Lenore found herself waiting for hours upon hours. Her impatience and distress grew. At times she thought about getting up and going to death's cave again. But she knew from what I had told her that death was a precarious thing. She feared angering it to the point that it would refuse to help her. She was scared of losing her love forever, and so she made herself stay put in her chair. Waiting tried her patience to the limit but it was all she could do. By the time the fire had died out, she had fallen asleep from the exhaustion of her sorrow.

In her dreams, I was there. Although she couldn't hear me, she could see the severe look on my face. It looked as though I was trying to warn her of something. She felt the pull of my hands on her wrists as I tried to lead her towards the door out of the castle. She tried to talk to me, to pull me towards her, but even as she did so, I persisted in leading her from the castle. Right before she woke from her dream, I finally spoke.

Run.

When Lenore woke up, she instinctively reached for her wrists and rubbed them. They felt sore. As she looked down at them, she noticed they were scratched and cut with what looked like talon marks.

"My love," a voice called from behind her.

It sounded hoarse and somewhat manic, but Lenore's heart leapt in her chest thinking that it was me and that the change in my voice was simply her disorientation from having been asleep. She jumped from the chair and turned around to reach for me. As she opened her eyes and saw who stood before her though, a feeling of horror like no other washed over her.

"Aren't you going to greet me, the love of your life, now returned from the dead to be by your side?"

Lenore's voice stuck in her throat. It felt like it was choking her. She tried to speak, but she couldn't. She was even too terrified to move. She stood paralysed in fear as the man walked towards her and took her hands in his.

"I know you are shocked. To be honest, I was too. But now I am only filled with happiness to be back with you, my love. Come, let us sit together and talk of all that we will do now that we have been given the gift of an eternity together."

The only thing that gave Lenore the strength to finally speak was her fury, which she now realised had been completely misdirected. It wasn't the woman who had orchestrated the death of her lover or the abomination which now stood before her; it was death.

"Edgar," Lenore whispered, nearly gagging on her own voice. "What are you doing here?"

Edgar's brow furrowed. He looked disappointed that Lenore didn't seem pleased to see him.

"I was brought back to you by a miracle," he said.

He squeezed her hands. She quickly drew them back.

"No," she said. "A miracle didn't bring you to the afterlife, death did."

"Well that seems a bit ridiculous doesn't it?" said Edgar, laughing. "*Death?* If death had anything to do with it then I would still be dead and not standing here in front of you. Was it you who wished for my return, my love?"

"No."

Edgar's troubled look turned to one of scorned rage. He spoke in the voice that she had tried so hard to forget.

"Tell me," he said. "Did you miss me while we were apart?"

Lenore couldn't answer. She feared that if she told Edgar the truth – that she wished he had stayed dead – he would be riled to the point of madness and would attempt to harm her in some way.

Edgar spoke in a sickeningly sweet voice that was much too exaggerated to be genuine.

"It's ok," he said. "I'm here now. Your troubles are over. I can see that you are at a loss for words. I expected as much. It is difficult to be reunited in love after so much time has passed."

"I never loved you," Lenore said.

She looked astonished that she had allowed those words to pass her lips, but something inside of her could no longer hold it in.

"Come now, that's not true. We loved each other beyond measure."

"No. I never loved you," she continued. "And you never loved me either. You were a sick and disturbed man, Edgar. You killed me. You killed me by squeezing the air from my lungs and crushing my rib cage beneath your hands. That isn't love; it's murder."

Edgar's eyes turned black with rage. It wasn't the same glistening endless black like my raven eyes. Instead, it was a dark pit of hatred and lunacy that threatened to suck up anything in its path.

"How dare you! I did love you Lenore – more than you should have been loved. And when you died, I mourned you gravely. In fact, I was so lost in sorrow and grief that my only companion was a dark bird which kept me company and tormented me with a word that rings in my ears even now… *Nevermore*."

"Nevermore?"

"Hush! Do not say it! I forbid it. That word will never be uttered again. That word wrapped itself around my mind until I was too confused to think clearly. I thought that bird was a message from you, but instead that damn raven was a curse."

Rainier, Lenore thought. She had to get me back. She tried to make a run for the door but was met with a piercing pain as Edgar snatched her by the hair and pulled her to the ground beside him.

"You're not leaving," he said. "Not again."

"Edgar, please," she begged. "Let me go."

Any small sliver of sanity or compassion that he may have once possessed was long gone. The back of his elbow cracked against her skull. The last thing Lenore saw was the floor coming closer.

When she woke up, she found herself tied to the side of the bedpost by a piece of thick rope that burned into her wrists.

"You're awake," said Edgar, smiling at her.

She wanted to scream at him, but she bit her tongue. She feared that insubordination would cost her consciousness again. So instead, she remained quiet and simply watched as he went about moving things around in the room. He moved the velvet armchair closer to the fire.

"Do you like the chair over here?" he asked. "I know how much you enjoyed the ambiance of the hearth while reading."

Lenore looked at him in disgust. He was clearly deranged. All she could think about was seeing me, even if it meant going back to talk to death. As Edgar continued to busily redecorate, it turned her stomach to see him acting as if all was well.

Annoyed that Lenore still hadn't answered his question, Edgar sauntered over to her and pulled the rope tighter, making it cut deeper into her wrists. He then added another rope; he looped it around her neck and affixed it to the side of his belt. The further he walked from her, the more the rope choked her.

"I'll ask again," he said, more sternly than before. "Do you like the chair here?"

He stood next to the chair's position near the fireplace but he quickly grew tired of hearing no answer and so proceeded to move again.

"Or here?" he said.

He pulled the chair alongside him as he walked further away towards the window. As he walked, the rope yanked at Lenore's throat until she had to tilt her head almost horizontally in order to breathe.

She tried to raise a finger to point back towards the position near the hearth.

"That's what I thought too," he said.

He grinned with satisfaction as he moved the chair over to the hearth. Lenore was able to breathe again thanks to the limp rope. It was a sick game of love and control that he played; one that she thought she would never have to endure again. She curled up on the bed and pretended to go to sleep in the hope that Edgar would stop talking to her. Instead of sleeping, she thought about me.

Death was supposed to be final; no thoughts, no feelings, no awareness unless summoned to the afterlife by one with the appropriate power and authority. I was special though. I was entirely aware of my existence in death. I was no longer in the afterlife and was definitely somewhere *else*. But even still, I existed. That alone was nothing short of a miracle.

It was dark and empty where I was. It wasn't distressing, or even uncomfortable. Darkness and solitude had always been enjoyable to me. Nevertheless, even my keen sense of sight couldn't make out anything around me. With my bird form trapped and broken in the afterlife, I walked around where I was in search of a way out. There was no other being there with me, which I found surprising.

Maybe everyone's death is their own private dark eternity alone, I thought.

I needed to get back to Lenore. Not only did I long for her, but I feared for her safety. I knew that things would not be right in the afterlife and I could sense that she was in danger. I wandered in a seemingly endless expanse for an indeterminate amount of time before I realised I was getting absolutely nowhere.

"How in the world do I get out of here and back to my love?" I called into the darkness.

"You don't," a voice answered.

I recognised that voice… It was death.

"Why am I here?" I asked death. "You and I have never crossed each other before. Why take me now?"

"I am not the one who took your life," death answered.

"Please," I begged. "You know I am smarter than to believe you had no part in this. And even if I didn't know that, I am smart enough to know that you can free me from here and place me back beside Lenore in my castle. So tell me, what is your reason?"

"Perhaps I just have a penchant for power."

"Power? You have the eternal power of death, what other power could you possibly want?"

"*Yours.*"

Suddenly, I realised what death had orchestrated. There was no one outside death's dominion now who could summon the dead into the afterlife, and no one to move between the land of the living and beyond. *Clever*, I thought. *But not clever enough.*

I laughed and then stood waiting for a reaction from death.

"What is it that you are laughing at? Are you not furious with me for having tricked you? You are stuck in here forever while your beautiful woman is in the afterlife with her living nightmare."

"Edgar?" I asked. "Why would you send Edgar there?"

"Oh, it was just a little added fun," death gloated.

I knew that I had to hurry. I had to outsmart death and get Lenore back. I couldn't let her endure atrocities that I dared not imagine at the hands of that man.

"I laughed because it is amusing how you think you have gained my power."

"Amusing or not, I have done so."

"No you haven't."

"What are you talking about?"

I could see death's movement in the deepest crevices of the darkness.

"I don't even have my abilities anymore. I gave them to Lenore before I arrived here. That morning, before you had me murdered, I gave them to her before I went on my flight."

"I don't believe you. There's no reason you would

have given her that power. And even if you had, why hasn't she used it to release you from death? You're lying. It's all too convenient to be true."

"Believe what you want, but it is true," I lied. "She hasn't released me because she doesn't know she holds the power to do so. But I will find it very satisfying to see your reaction when she realises what she is capable of. You haven't stopped my power; you've simply left it in the hands of the one woman who now despises you more than anything."

Death was silent. I wasn't sure if I had been successful in my deception and trickery. I called out to death several times but there was no answer, for it had left to go and resolve the problem it now thought existed in the afterlife. So blinded by power, death resolved to just kill Lenore and end any threat of outside power that he could not control. There were rules to abide by, of course. A life could not just be plucked by death on impulse, not even from the afterlife. But death didn't care about the rules anymore.

When death swept into the castle and found Edgar hovering over Lenore's body as she pretended to be asleep, it took less than a second for it to deliver a striking blow through the heart that plunged Lenore back into a permanent death. Edgar stood over her body looking aghast that his love would be lost yet a second time.

As soon as Lenore was killed, she found herself standing in blackness. A hand reached out to touch hers. She was scared and startled, but when I spoke, all of her fear subsided.

"It's ok," I said. "You are here with me."

She grabbed me and pulled me close to her.

"How is it that we are here together?" she asked. "When I was in death before, I was alone."

"We will never be apart again," I answered her. "I tricked death into leaving its own cavern to kill you, which sent you here to me. You see, the dead are not the only ones who have to get permission to move. When death left, its power to return remained here with me."

"Do you mean that death is stuck in the afterlife now?"

"Yes."

"And what of us? How do we get back to the castle?"

"We don't. We can't stay there anymore," I explained. "But there is more than one afterlife; there are several. I have seen them on my flights. I have searched for other places and ways to get to them. If I can just find my bird form in here, then I can take us to one of them."

Lenore helped me search through the darkness until we were able to find my broken feathered form on the ground. She picked up the lifeless bird in her hands and held it up to me.

"How do we fix this?" she asked.

I closed her fingers around the lifeless bird and gently pushed it towards her chest.

"Say my name," I said.

Lenore closed her eyes and soulfully held the lifeless raven against her heart.

"Rainier," she said.

The blackness around us changed to more of a smoky grey. Soon there was enough visibility that she could see me transform from man to bird as the feathery corpse dissolved from her hands. I swirled around her, and she reached out to touch my wing. The darkness around us faded away and she found herself standing in the bedroom of a different – yet equally striking – castle. She looked at me and said my name once more. Once again, I transformed into a man, confidently standing before her.

"Where are we?" she asked.

"Our new home," I said proudly. "No one will find us here, not even death."

"How is that possible?" she asked.

"Because death has found itself a new preoccupation. I have to go somewhere for only a very short time. I will be back before you even notice my absence, I promise."

Although Lenore was still confused, I kissed her softly. I assured her that I would be back and that she should settle herself in our new home.

As I flew back towards my previous castle, I thought about how clever I had been to outwit death. Because of the mistake death had made in leaving the cave, it would now be trapped inside the very place in which it had killed Lenore: my castle. And, since there was no one to call Edgar back into death, they would be trapped there together for all time.

I knew that I needed to move on, but I felt justified in seeking to relish this last bit of vengeance that I was due. I flew in through the open window and saw the shadow of death furiously stalking the corners of the castle. I saw Edgar sitting in the dark velvet chair descending once more into madness over the loss of Lenore for the second time. I flapped my wings and cawed as loudly as I could, circling the room near the high ceilings. Edgar looked up and threw his hands up to curse me, and death called out to me in hatred.

"When I get out of this entrapment, I will come for you," death bellowed at me. "I will pull you into a death so deep and dark that you will never escape from it. What do you think about that, raven?"

I swooped down and circled around death just once. Before flying back out of the castle window for the last time to head back to my love, I called back the single word that would haunt both Edgar and death for all of eternity.

"Nevermore!"

****

www.ingramcontent.com/pod-product-compliance
Lightning Source LLC
Chambersburg PA
CBHW061220210726
48294CB00006B/1914